LITTLE SIMON
An imprint of Simon & Schuster Children's Publishing Division
1230 Avenue of the Americas, New York, New York 10020
This Little Simon hardcover edition September 2021

LITTLE SIMON is a registered trademark of Simon & Schuster, Inc., and associated colophon is a trademark of Simon & Schuster, Inc.
For information about special discounts for bulk purchases, please contact Simon & Schuster Special Sales at 1-866-506-1949 or
business@simonandschuster.com. The Simon & Schuster Speakers Bureau can bring authors to your live event. For more information
or to book an event contact the Simon & Schuster Speakers Bureau at 1-866-248-3049 or visit our website at www.simonspeakers.com.
Designed by Chani Yammer
Manufactured in China 0621 SCP
10 9 8 7 6 5 4 3 2 1
A previous edition of this book has been cataloged with the Library of Congress.
ISBN 978-1-5344-8445-0
ISBN 978-1-5344-0086-3 (eBook)

THE NIGHT BEFORE CHRISTMAS

By Clement C. Moore   Illustrated by Antonio Javier Caparo

LITTLE SIMON

New York London Toronto Sydney New Delhi

'Twas the night before Christmas,
when all through the house
not a creature was stirring,
not even a mouse.

The stockings were hung by the chimney with care, in hopes that St. Nicholas soon would be there.

The children were nestled all snug in their beds
while visions of sugarplums danced in their heads.

And Mamma in her kerchief and I in my cap
had just settled our brains
for a long winter's nap.

When out on the lawn there arose such a clatter,
I sprang from my bed to see what was the matter.

Away to the window I flew like a flash,
tore open the shutters, and threw up the sash.

The moon on the breast of the new-fallen snow
gave a lustre of midday to objects below.

When what to my wondering eyes did appear
but a miniature sleigh and eight tiny reindeer.

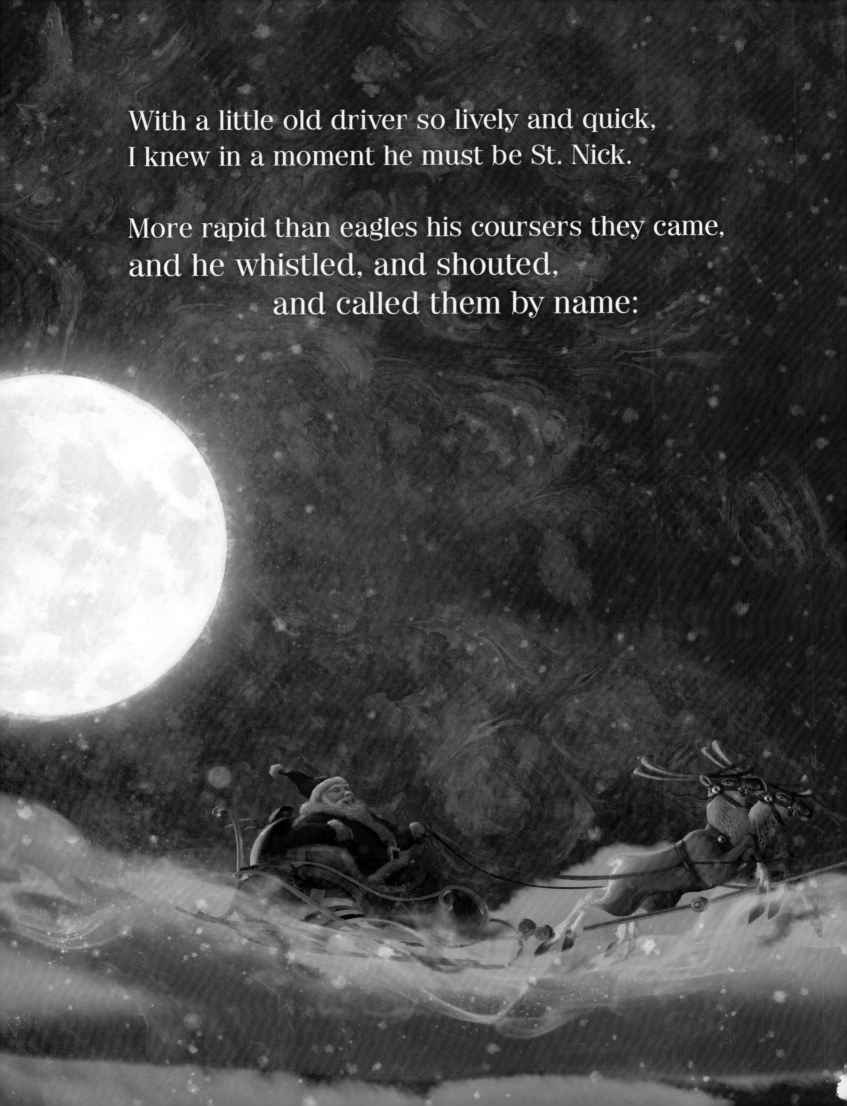

With a little old driver so lively and quick,
I knew in a moment he must be St. Nick.

More rapid than eagles his coursers they came,
and he whistled, and shouted,
and called them by name:

"Now, Dasher! Now, Dancer!
Now, Prancer and Vixen!
On, Comet! On, Cupid! On, Donner and Blitzen!"

"To the top of the porch! To the top of the wall!
Now dash away! Dash away! Dash away all!"

As leaves that before the wild hurricane fly,
when they meet with an obstacle, mount to the sky;
so up to the housetop the coursers they flew
with the sleigh full of toys, and St. Nicholas, too.

And then, in a twinkling, I heard on the roof
the prancing and pawing of each little hoof.

As I drew in my head
and was turning around,
down the chimney St. Nicholas came
with a bound.
He was dressed all in fur,
from his head to his foot,
and his clothes were all tarnished
with ashes and soot.

Dear Santa:

A bundle of toys he had flung on his back,
and he looked like a peddler just opening his pack.

His eyes—how they twinkled! His dimples, how merry!
His cheeks were like roses, his nose like a cherry!
His droll little mouth was drawn up like a bow,
and the beard on his chin was as white as the snow.

The stump of a pipe he held tight in his teeth,
and the smoke, it encircled his head like a wreath.
He had a broad face and a little round belly
that shook when he laughed, like a bowl full of jelly.

He was chubby and plump, a right jolly old elf,
and I laughed when I saw him, in spite of myself;
a wink of his eye and a twist of his head
soon gave me to know I had nothing to dread.

He spoke not a word,
but went straight to his work
and filled all the stockings,
then turned with a jerk.

And laying his finger aside of his nose,
and giving a nod, up the chimney he rose.

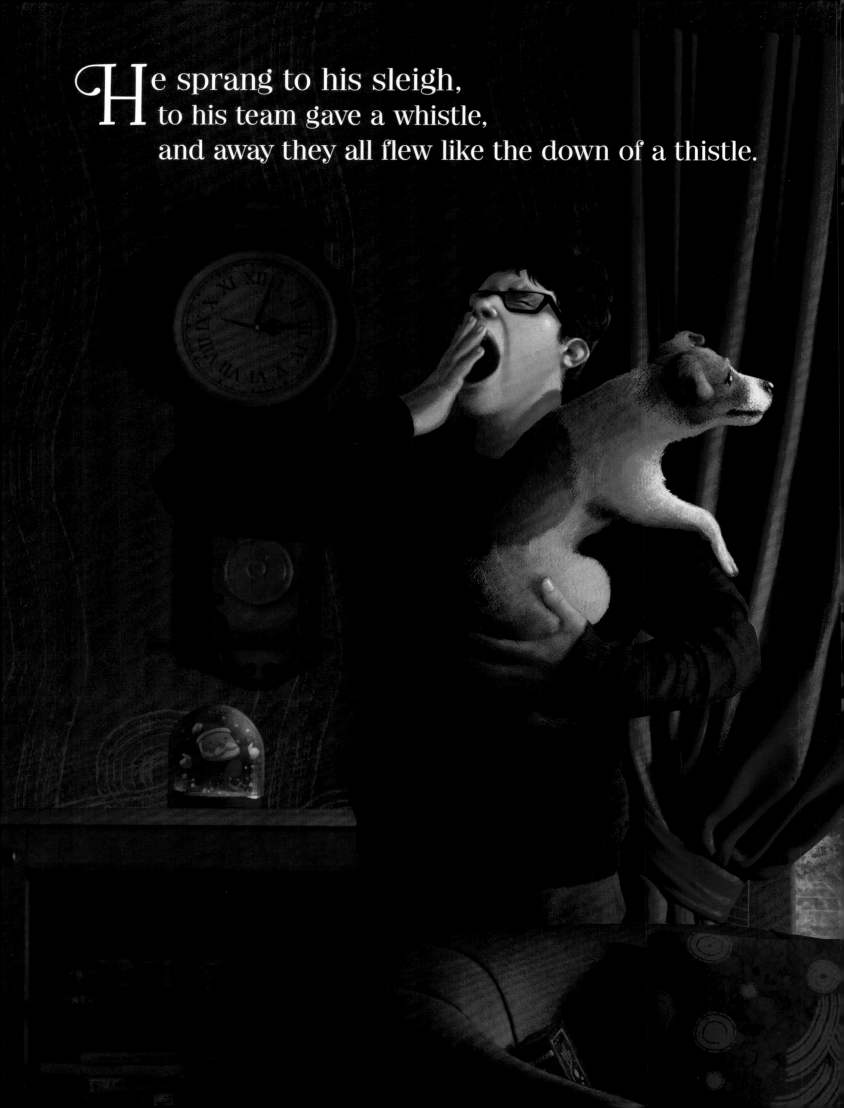

He sprang to his sleigh,
to his team gave a whistle,
and away they all flew like the down of a thistle.